MIGHTY WORRIER
AND THE ALIEN INVASION

WILF THE MIGHTY WORRIER

AND THE ALIEN INVASION

Georgia Pritchett

Illustrated by
JAMIE LITTLER

Quercus

QUERCUS CHILDREN'S BOOKS

First published in Great Britain in 2016 by Hodder and Stoughton

1 3 5 7 9 10 8 6 4 2

A CIP catalogue record for this book
is available from the British Library.

ISBN 978 1 78429 874 6

Printed and bound in Great Britain
by Clays

The paper and board used in this book are
made from wood from responsible sources.

MIX
Paper from
responsible sources
FSC® C104740

Quercus Children's Books
An imprint of
Hachette Children's Group
Part of Hodder and Stoughton
Carmelite House
50 Victoria Embankment
London EC4Y 0DZ

An Hachette UK Company
www.hachette.co.uk
www.hachettechildrens.co.uk

For my boys

Chapter One
PLEASE EAT AFTER READING

NOT YOU AGAIN!

I thought I told you before!

This book is only for special people. This book has **TOP SECRET** information. The **TOPPEST SECRETEST** information. So after you've read it, you should really **DESTROY** it. I recommend eating it with some cheese and pickle.

If you don't like the taste of book (or you are on some kind of paper-free diet), tear each page into a thousand pieces and then feed each teeny tiny piece to a woodworm. **(Warning: that could take ages.)**

Or, if you don't like woodworms, tear each page into a hundred pieces and make a teeny tiny paper aeroplane with each bit. Then give each paper aeroplane to an ant and ask each ant to climb up somewhere very high and throw their paper aeroplane as far as they can.

Or, if you're no good at making paper aeroplanes, then you could tear each page into a thousand pieces and then put an incy wincy blob of glue on each one and stick it to a bumblebee's bottom and then they will fly off and the pages will be scattered to the wind.

On second thoughts, that won't work because at the end of the day, the bees will all come home to their hive and if they all lined up in the right order then the bee-keeper might be able to read the book off their bottoms. And we don't want any old bee-keeper knowing these **TOP SECRET** things – that could be dangerous.

OK. So is the coast clear? Then I will begin.

So, you know Wilf? Yes you **dooooo**, yes you **dooooo**.

That boy at school with pingy ears and scruffly hair and a head so full of ideas it's like teeny tiny fireworks going off in his head. Yes, him! And he has a little sister called Dot who is very grubby and sticky. She is basically a big smell and a loud noise trapped in a small body.

Well, Wilf saved the Universe last week. Yes he did. And he experienced an alien invasion. And he also ate jelly for the first time. Which sounds less exciting, but if you know Wilf and know his very strong feelings about jelly, it is actually pretty impressive.

This is how the **whole kerfuffle** started. Wilf and Dot had been having a very busy day. Wilf had written out his most up-to-date list of worries and laminated it. They were –

Suits of armour
Bald cats
Aliens laying eggs in him
Being made into soup

Meanwhile Dot had been seeing which foods make a sound if you throw them on to the floor.

A potato – yes.

Jelly – no.

An entire tub of cake sprinkles – yes. In fact, the best noise of all, but they made the floor rather skiddy.

Next, Wilf fetched his piggy bank to see how much money he had saved. He had quite a lot because he had been doing odd jobs for his evil next-door-neighbour Alan – like mowing his lawn and cleaning his windows and polishing his moustache.

Wilf carefully counted what was inside – twenty-two coins, a chocolate button and a tiddlywink which Dot must have put in there. Wilf was very excited – because he only needed twenty-two coins to buy the **VERY SPECIAL THING** he had been saving up for.

And FINALLY he had twenty-one coins.

Hang on.

A minute ago he had twenty-two coins. Where has the other coin gone? It was here just now. Dot! Open your mouth! Yes, right now. Open it. There's the coin. Thank you. You can eat the chocolate button but not the tiddlywi—

Too late. Gosh, aren't tiddlywinks crunchy? Anyway, where was I?

You see, Wilf had decided that he wanted to be an astronaut when he grew up. Either that or an astronomer, except Wilf couldn't actually say 'astronomer' and Wilf thought it was probably important to be able to say the job that you do.

So in order to be an astronaut or an astronowhatsit, Wilf thought that it would be a good idea to have a telescope to look at the stars.

And THAT was the **VERY SPECIAL THING** he went to the shops to buy.

And THAT was where this **whole kerfuffle** started.

Chapter Two
BEST SERVED
WITH CUSTARD

The next day, Wilf was in the garden playing with his new telescope. It was amazing. If you looked through one end, everything was very

CLOSE.

And if you looked through the other end, everything was very

far away.

And if you let Dot near it, you couldn't see anything at all because it got all sticky and smeary.

"What are you doing?" asked Alan, peering over the garden fence.

"I'm playing with my brand-new telescope," explained Wilf. "It's so powerful, I can see right up into space."

"Space is boring," said Alan. "It's just a load of space."

"Well, actually space is very interesting and there are billions of stars and Earth is one of the smallest planets in the Universe," Wilf said.

Wilf tried to explain using different pieces of fruit to show how the planets orbit around the sun. He got an orange for the sun and then a walnut for Mercury because that is the smallest. And then he got a kiwi for Earth because there is a lot of green on Earth, and then a big red apple for Mars – but while he was getting a big red apple, Kevin Phillips, Alan's right-hand man, came sniffing around and tried to eat the planet Mercury. And then Dot ate Mars and it all went a bit wrong.

"Ah-ha!" said Alan. "That gives me an idea!"

"What is it?" asked Wilf excitedly.

"Firstly, to eat the sun," said Alan, taking the orange. "But then to do something much more thrilling. And **EVIL**."

Over the next few days, Wilf worried a LOT about what Alan's evil plan might be. But he didn't have time to worry too much because he was SO busy. Alan was asking him to do even more odd jobs than usual such as –

Buying rocket fuel
Buying more rocket fuel
Buying more rocket fuel
Buying more rocket fuel
Buying more rocket fuel
Buying some sweeties
Buying more rocket fuel

Wilf didn't know what Alan was up to. But it was bound to be something bad.

He decided to distract himself from his worrying thoughts by looking through his telescope again. But hang on – where was his telescope? It wasn't in any of its usual places like on his desk or in Dot's mouth. Where could it be?

He looked out of the window and saw Alan and Kevin Phillips playing fetch with a stick. Kevin Phillips was running round and round Alan while Alan shouted, **"Drop! Drop it! Drop! Drop! Drop it, I said!"** over and over again.

Finally Kevin got dizzy and dropped the stick. Except it wasn't a stick. It was Wilf's telescope!

"Good boy!" said Alan. "Come on, let's take it inside!"

And with that Alan and Kevin bounded off
into Alan's house, taking Wilf's telescope with
them.

Wilf gasped. "So THAT was his evil plan!
To steal my telescope!" he said. (Which is of
course absolute tosh and nonsense. What a
nincompoop. Don't tell Wilf I said that.)

Wilf decided he HAD to get his telescope
back!

There was just one problem. If he went round to Alan's house, he would have to walk right past the new suit of armour that Alan had put by the front door. Wilf was scared of suits of armour. He was worried they might chase him in a clattery clanky way.

Wilf went and got his latest '**HOW TO STOP WORRYING**' leaflet. It had lots of suggestions of things to do that might help. Wilf looked at **NUMBER ONE**.

1) Draw a picture of the thing you are worried about.

Wilf drew a suit of armour.
NUMBER TWO said:

2) Think of the worst-case scenario.

Wilf thought. What could be worse than being chased by a suit of armour? Not much. But possibly being chased by a suit

of armour with a bald cat. Wilf was scared of bald cats. Because they made Wilf feel all blarghhhhhhhhhh.

Wilf drew his worst-case scenario.

Even looking at the picture made Wilf feel wobbly, so he did a few casual hops to make himself feel better. Then he read on.

NUMBER THREE said:

3) Think of a plan of action if the worst-case scenario happens.

Wilf thought.

If a suit of armour with a bald cat tried to chase him, Wilf would give the cat a bowl of milk to distract it, then he would skate away on his roller skates as fast as he could. And if the suit of armour caught up with him, he would tie his skipping rope round its clattery clanking legs to stop it.

Wilf drew this.

He put on his roller skates, picked up his skipping rope and poured a bowl of milk. Then he and Dot set off for Alan's house to get his telescope back.

Chapter Three
DELICIOUS WITH KETCHUP

Wilf glided along silently on his roller skates. Dot padded along next to him in her Babygro. The only sound was the gentle lapping of the milk in the bowl. Plus Dot sucking noisily on her dummy and blowing off with every step.

They reached Alan's front door. It was ajar, which is a funny way of saying it was a little bit open. Wilf gently pushed it.

Creeeeeeeeeeaaaaaaaaaaaaaaaaaaaaak

went the door, opening just enough to reveal the dark suit of armour, looming in the hallway.

Wilf shuddered.

Dot burped.

Wilf stepped into the hallway with wobbly legs and skated quickly past the suit of armour. He looked back anxiously. Was it watching him? Was it following him? Were its clanky legs about to clatter after him? No. It was just standing there, looking a bit dusty.

And its foot was looking a bit snotty and dribbly.

That must have been Dot.

CLANK! went the suit of armour.

Wilf leapt into the air and let out a very high-pitched squeal.

But it was just Dot hammering the suit of armour with her toy tractor.

Phew.

So now all Wilf had to do was find his telescope.

First, they looked in Alan's bedroom. But all they found was a lot of dirty pants.

Next, they checked Kevin Phillips's basket. But all they found were five tennis balls, twelve sticks, eighteen socks, an empty packet of biscuits and thirty-seven pebbles.

No telescope.

It must be somewhere! thought Wilf

Hang on a minute, what's that over there?

No, not that, that's an umbrella. There, over there.

No, that's a torch. Under there, look, in that welly boot – the telescope!

Wilf and Dot made their way towards it.

"**Shhh**," said Wilf to Dot.

"**Shhh**," said Dot to Wilf.

"**Shhh,**" said Alan to Kevin Phillips who had been watching them all along.

"IT'S YOUR LUCKY DAY!"

yelled Alan.

Wilf leapt up in the air again. When he landed his legs skated in opposite directions, which was jolly uncomfortable.

"Is it?" asked Wilf. He wasn't convinced.

"Yes. It is," said Alan. "If you want to be obliterated."

"It wasn't on my list of things to do," admitted Wilf.

"Well, it is on mine. Here. Number 27 – obliterate a small child. Or two. Even better. Step this way."

Alan led them to a huge GLASS chamber.

"Since you destroyed my **Big Gun Thingy** (Book One) AND my **Big Cannon Thingy** (Book Two) AND my **Bouncy Explodey Snake Bomb** (Book Three), I have built myself a brand-new weapon. Behold! My brand-new **Dangerous Obliterating Lightning Laser**, or my **D.O.L.L** for short. Kevin? Pass me my **DOLL**."

Wilf tried not to laugh.

"What?" said Alan crossly. "What's wrong with that?"

"It's fine, it's fine. It just makes you sound like you might be a three-year-old," said Wilf.

"Well, that wasn't what I was going for," said Alan. "In that case, I will change the name. I will call it the **Dangerous Ultimate Machine for Melting You**. Or **D.U.M.M.Y.** Now Kevin, pass me my **dummy**..." said Alan.

Wilf tried not to laugh.

"What?" said Alan.

"It's just you said dummy..." explained Wilf.

"Not good?" asked Alan.

"It makes you sound a bit babyish," said Wilf.

"Well, we can't have that," said Alan.

"Why don't you just call it your **Big Laser Zappy Thingy**," suggested Wilf. "Then we'll all know where we are."

"Good idea," said Alan. "The only problem is, it isn't actually that big. You see, I bought the parts online and they turned out to be much smaller than I thought they would be."

"It is annoying when that happens," said Wilf sympathetically.

"I know. I was hoping to destroy the whole world but it's nowhere near big enough so I'll just have to make do with destroying you for the time being," said Alan.

And with that he shoved Wilf and Dot into the chamber and closed the door.

Wilf was scared! He didn't want to be obliterated. He wished he was at home, hoovering or organising his sock drawer or baking a cake, but he wasn't: he and Dot were trapped and he had to do something! He had a great big old worry and then he had a great big old think and then he thought so hard that his brain got cross with him and then he had an idea.

"Before you obliterate us," said Wilf. "May I say a few last words?"

"Oh, very well. If you must," grumped Alan and he stomped back into the chamber. "What is it?" he said gruffly.

"Um...**Ischial callosities**," said Wilf.

"I beg your pardon?" said Alan.

"**Ischial callosities**," repeated Wilf. "Those are my last words," he explained. "Because they're my favourite words."

"Why are they your favourite words?" asked Alan.

"Because they sound like they mean something terribly important but actually they're just a very posh way of saying a monkey's bottom. Which is a bit rude. So that makes me laugh."

"You made me come all the way back in here so you could say monkey's bottom?" asked Alan irritably.

"Yes. A little bit," admitted Wilf. "Oh, and also to do this."

And with that, he threw the bowl of milk into Alan's face.

"Aaargh! Milk! I'm **lactose intolerant!**" screamed Alan. "Kevin! Obliterate them!"

Kevin lolloped towards the controls, but just as he reached the lever, Wilf threw his skipping rope round the end of the laser and spun it away from him and Dot.

"**Zzzzzzzapppppppp!**" went the laser, through the door of the chamber and out into the hallway.

And the suit of armour was obliterated.

Things had worked out very well indeed for Wilf. But he didn't have time to celebrate – he had to escape. He scooped Dot up, skated out of the glass chamber and through the front door and clattered down the path in a clattery clanky way, until Alan's cries of "I'm going to get terrible wind after this!" got fainter and fainter.

It was only once Wilf and Dot were home and safe and Wilf was doing a little hoppy dance of celebration that he suddenly stopped mid-hop. He realized he hadn't actually got his telescope back! And he also realized that he couldn't let Alan get away with it. And **THAT** is where this **whole kerfuffle** **REALLY** started.

Chapter Four

I'M A BIT FULL NOW — CAN I PUT THIS CHAPTER IN THE FRIDGE AND EAT IT LATER?

"I see Alan's had a loft extension," said Wilf's mum the next day over breakfast. "I hope he got planning permission."

"Nng," said Wilf, which is the only noise you can really make when grown-ups start droning on about planning permission or bin day or traffic or what the weather used to be like in the olden days.

"Anyway, must put the bins out," said Wilf's mum.

"Nng," said Wilf.

"And then I'm off. Don't want to get caught in traffic," she added.

"Nng," said Wilf.

"Can you believe the weather?" exclaimed Wilf's mum. "Wasn't like this when I was a child."

And with that she was gone, stopping only to shout through the letterbox that Wilf had his shoes on the wrong feet.

"I'm not wearing shoes," said Wilf. "These are my actual feet."

"I'm reminding you for later. In case I don't see you," shouted Wilf's mum.

Wilf looked out of the window. Loft extension? That was no loft extension! Alan's house was now hundreds and hundreds of metres taller than it had been. What on EARTH was he up to?

Wilf and Dot went out into the garden. Wilf peeped through the fence. He could see Alan talking to his robot, Mark III, who was built to do his every bidding.

"Right, Mark III, listen very carefully, because I have an excellent new evil plan which is to become **RULER OF THE UNIVERSE** and then to destroy it. Or possibly the other way round."

Wilf was staggerblasted. His hair went all hot and his stomach badoinged and his knees wanted to bend the wrong way. So THAT was Alan's evil plan! Stealing telescopes was bad enough – but this was a LOT worse. Wilf wanted to run and he wanted to hide and he wanted to knit a big nest that he could curl up in, but he couldn't do that because he needed to stay and listen to Alan.

"I have something to show you," said Alan to Mark III. "Follow me."

"I'm busy," moaned Mark III.

"It won't take a minute," snapped Alan.

"Can't someone else do it?" whined Mark III.

"No. They can't!" exclaimed Alan.

"Why me?" complained Mark III.

"Because you're my robot!" said Alan. "And I built you to do my every bidding."

Mark III tutted. "Typical!" he muttered. "It's so unfair."

"Right. Come over here," said Alan. "And if it's not too much trouble, try to behave a bit more like the sophisticated high-tech robot that you are."

"Fine. I will," sulked Mark III. "In that case, for security reasons, you will need to create a password before I can do anything else," said Mark III.

"Very well. **Alan**. That's my password," snapped Alan.

"Your password is too short," replied Mark III.

"All right. **Alanistheruleroftheuniverse**," huffed Alan.

"Your password is too long," said Mark III.

"Drat. What about **Alanistheruler**?" asked Alan.

"Your password should have numbers in it," said Mark III.

"**Alanistheruler1**, then," said Alan crossly.

"Your password should have a mixture of upper case and lower case letters," said Mark III.

"Fine," spat Alan. "**AlanIsTheRuler1**."

"Your password should not contain your name," said Mark III.

"**Drat drat drat!**" yelled Alan, jumping up and down.

"Your password is accepted," said Mark III.

"No, but wait – that wasn't my password! I want to change it!"

"Your password is now set."

"But it didn't have numbers or any of the things you said!" screeched Alan.

Mark III said nothing.

"Fine. Fine. Just come on," said Alan. "And you Kevin."

Mark III and Kevin followed Alan towards a very long ladder that was leaning against the new very tall tower on Alan's house. They started climbing.

"This could be the perfect moment to get my telescope back," whispered Wilf to Dot.

"Bottom!" shouted Dot. She had just learnt a rude word and was using it wherever possible.

"Let's go, while they're not looking," said Wilf.

"Two bottoms!" shouted Dot, presumably because that was twice as rude.

"Come on," said Wilf, "through this gap in the fence."

"Five bottoms!" replied Dot.

"Yes. Very good," said Wilf.

They crawled through the gap in the fence and tiptoed (not easy when your knees are trying to bend the wrong way) towards the welly boot where they had last seen the telescope. Just then they heard a very loud rumbling.

"Oh dear," said Wilf. "Is that your bottom, Dot? Is that what you were trying to say?"

Dot looked down at her nappy expectantly.

The ground began to shake.

"Oh, Dot. Have you been eating blueberries?" said Wilf anxiously.

The windows in Alan's house began to rattle.

Suddenly, the roof opened to reveal the nose of an enormous space rocket. At the same time, huge jets of flame burst out through the front door.

Wilf and Dot looked up.

Alan, Mark III and Kevin Phillips were sitting in the cockpit of the rocket. Alan was holding Wilf's telescope. Alan turned to Kevin Phillips and yelled, "According to Wilf's Fruit Map, we need to set co-ordinates for a big red apple."

And with an enormous roar, the rocket zoomed up into space.

Wilf and Dot turned to look at each other.

"Blinking heck!" exclaimed Wilf.

"Ten bottoms and another bottom!" agreed Dot.

And THAT'S ACTUALLY where this **whole kerfuffle** started.

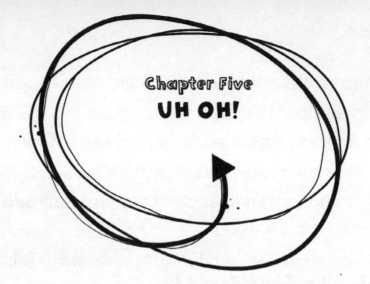

Chapter Five
UH OH!

The next few days were very difficult. Wilf was worried. Plus he missed his telescope. And, it has to be said, he missed Alan too. It was quiet without him. Too quiet. Alan could be jolly good company when he wasn't trying to destroy the world.

Wilf passed the time as best he could. He hopped. He whistled. He knitted. He sorted out his sock drawer. He hopped some more.

He hid under his duvet.

In fact, he was busy hiding under his duvet when he heard a tremendous noise. It's hard to describe really. (Yes, I know it's my job to describe things but I find it very difficult.) It was loud. And it was **SCREECHY**. But a sort of deep screech. And it was **RUMBLY** but in a high-pitched way. But most of all, it was **CRASHY**.

Wilf crawled from the bed, still under his duvet, and peeped out of the window. The space rocket was next to Alan's house, looking rather grubby and dirty. It was still very, very tall, but not quite as tall as before – because now the nose cone was all zig-zaggy.

"Alan's back!" yelled Wilf to Dot excitedly, and they ran outside to their garden.

"You're back!" said Wilf, over the fence.

"Hmm?" said Alan. "Oh yes. Yes."

"What was space like?" asked Wilf breathlessly.

"Fine," said Alan, a bit sulkily. "Just, you know, spacey."

Wilf looked over at Alan's zig-zaggy rocket.

"What happened to your rocket?" asked Wilf.

"Nothing," Alan lied. "It was always like that."

"Are you sure?" asked Wilf. "I thought it was smooth and pointy?"

"No, no. It was always crumpled."

"Are you going to go back into space?" asked Wilf.

"Nah, there was nothing up there," said Alan.

"Yeah," agreed Mark III, "it was boring. We couldn't find any apples or oranges or kiwis."

"I don't think I'll bother with taking over the Universe," said Alan. "I think I'm going to sort out my sock drawer instead."

This was music to Wilf's ears. "I love sorting out my sock drawer. I could help you if you like! Are you thinking of sorting it by colour, thickness or length?"

But before Alan could answer, there was a tremendous

and a huge shadow fell over the garden.

Wilf and Alan looked up. Hovering over their heads was a ginormous **ALIEN SPACESHIP**.

I suppose you'll want to know what it looked like. So annoying. You know I hate describing things. It was **HUGE**, all right? And I mean, really **GINORMOUSLY BIG**. Imagine something **HUMUNGOUS** and that's how big it was. No, **BIGGER** than that. **BIGGER** than that. Much **BIGGER** than that. You're just not imagining **BIGLY** enough. Try again. OK. Imagine if a whale was a spaceship. But a different shape. And a different colour. And not at all whale-like. It looked a bit like that. But different. Got that? Good.

Then suddenly there was a very loud

noise.

Do I have to describe that as well? This is

exhausting! Well, it sounded a bit like if a huge giant was trying to play a walrus like a trumpet. But different from that. It sounded a bit like if a T-Rex had eaten too many baked beans and tried to do a quiet blow off but it came out more noisily than he'd expected. But different from that too. Actually, do you know what it sounded **EXACTLY** like? Like a hatch opening on a giant spaceship. Because that's what it was.

Wilf and Alan looked up, rooted to the spot. Kevin Phillips was almost rooted to the spot, but just slowly scooting backwards on his bottom.

"Bus!" Dot shouted, pointing happily.

A small speaker descended from the hatch. There was a loud crackle and then they heard a gurgly alien voice.

"We come from
the planet Mars. We are
looking for Alan,"

gurgled the voice.

"That's Alan!" said Alan, pointing to Wilf.
And with that Alan ran into his house and hid.

Before Wilf could run anywhere, a large ramp started descending from the spaceship into his garden.

Wilf was terrified. He was scared of aliens and he was particularly scared of an alien attaching itself to his face and laying eggs in him. He wished he had stayed under his duvet, but he hadn't: he was here and he had to do something! He grabbed his **HOW TO STOP WORRYING** leaflet from his back pocket. **NUMBER FOUR** said –

4) Try counting backwards slowly.

Wilf started trying to count backwards.

"T-t-t-twenty," he stuttered. "N-n-n-nineteen. Eighteen...seconds until aliens come down the ramp and attach themselves to my face and lay eggs in me," he wobbled.

This wasn't really helping.

"Seventeen seconds until…

aaaaaaarrrrrrgggggghhhhhhh," yelped Wilf, as three aliens began walking slowly and blobbily towards him.

Now, you're going to want to know what the aliens looked like, aren't you? This is relentless!

Right, well, they were very green, very blobby and they had lots and lots of eyes. Got that? No, a much brighter green than that. And even blobbier. And loads more eyes.

"Sixteen seconds until three blobby green aliens blob towards me and lay eggs in me," whimpered Wilf.

This was not helping **AT ALL**.

In fact, it was making it worse.

So Wilf had a great big old worry and then he had a great big old think and then he thought so hard that his brain almost got tangled in a knot and then he had an idea!

He rushed to his shed and got his Spider-Man mask so that his face was covered up.

He also got his jar of tadpoles so that if the aliens felt like laying eggs, they might do so in the jar.

Finally, he found a big rock. If the worst came to the worst, he would throw the rock at the aliens and run as fast as he could.

"Greetings!" said the biggest alien, when Wilf returned. "I am Bok."

"And I am Mok," said the middle-sized alien.

"And I am Lok," squeaked the littlest alien.

"H-h-h-h-h-hello," said Wilf in a wobbly voice.

"Hello, Alan," said the aliens. "We followed you home by using this excellent contraption you left behind."

"My telescope!" said Wilf excitedly.

"Yes, Alan. Your telescope," said Bok. "And your rocket," he added, pointing to the smoking crumpled wreck next to them. "I don't think I need to tell you that you are in a LOT of trouble."

Wilf gulped a very loud gulp. "The thing is, I'm not actually Alan," he explained. "My name is W-w-w-w-w-w-w-w-wilf."

"Oh. Hello, W-w-w-w-w-w-w-w-wilf," said the aliens.

"I would shake your, erm, hands, but mine are rather full," said Wilf, juggling the rock and the tadpoles.

"How did you know?" asked Bok.

"Know what?" said Wilf.

"That this is our favourite delicacy," said Bok, taking the rock and chomping it down in two big bites. "And this is our favourite drink," he added, grabbing the jar of tadpoles and drinking it down in one.

"Er…lucky guess?" said Wilf.

"Now, before we go any further," said Mok, "we want to make something clear. We absolutely refuse to lay eggs in you. We know what you humans are like, always travelling to other planets and wanting us to lay eggs in you, but we've had enough of it. Do you understand?"

"Yes!" said Wilf, very relieved. "In that case, I can take this off." He removed his Spider-Man mask.

"**Argh!** His face has fallen off!" said Lok, and then he fainted.

"Sorry about that," said Bok. "Lok worries a lot."

"And he is scared of you," said Mok.

"There's no need to be scared of me," Wilf assured them. "I worry a lot too. In fact, I have a leaflet that Lok might find useful."

"That's very kind," said Bok, taking the leaflet and fanning Lok with it, "but first, please take us to your leader."

"When you say 'leader'," said Wilf, "what exactly do you mean?"

"The SUPREME LEADER OF EARTH, of course," said Mok.

Wilf started to explain that there wasn't a SUPREME LEADER OF EARTH, but he was interrupted by Alan arriving in his garden. He was wearing a paper crown (from a Christmas cracker) and a curtain draped around his shoulders like a cape. "I am the SUPREME LEADER OF EARTH!" boomed Alan. (Actually, Alan doesn't boom, does he? It was more of a loud whine.)

"I beg your pardon?" said Bok.

"I, Alan, am the SUPREME LEADER OF EARTH," repeated Alan.

Bok and Mok laughed. Lok opened his many many eyes and struggled blobbily to his feet.

"You are very funny," they said. "And you have lovely curtains."

"No, but I really am," insisted Alan.

"No, you are not," said the aliens as politely as they could.

"All right, all right, I may not be the SUPREME LEADER OF EARTH right now, but I will be very, very soon – just as soon as I get my new BIGGER laser zapper thingy out of the packaging. I mean, how do they expect people to open these things? If I was an old lady living on my own, I'd have no chance."

"It is impossible that you could ever be the SUPREME LEADER," said Bok.

Alan looked very upset. "But why?" he asked, stamping his foot (which made his paper crown fall off).

"Because you are a man," explained Mok. "SUPREME LEADERS can only be women."

"Absolute poppycock," said Alan. "On Earth, ALL the rulers are men. I mean there's the odd woman occasionally, but only by accident."

The aliens were amazed. "Is he making a funny joke?" they asked Wilf.

"No, it's true," said Wilf, "they are usually men."

"But why?" gasped the aliens.

"I don't really know," admitted Wilf. "It seems unfair."

"I'll tell you why," said Alan. "It's because men are stronger."

"Ha ha ha ha ha ha," said the aliens. "No really, tell us why."

"It's the truth," fumed Alan. "Men ARE stronger."

"What? ALL Earth men are stronger than

ALL Earth women?"

"Well, no," admitted Alan. "But some men are stronger than some women."

"But what does that mean?" asked Mok, still perplexed.

"Well, men can, you know…undo stiff jars, and things."

"Ha ha ha ha ha ha," said the aliens.

Alan was getting annoyed. "Not just that, but they can lift heavy suitcases as well."

"Ha ha ha ha ha! Heavy suitcases!" said the aliens. They were really enjoying themselves now. "What else? What else?"

"Well, men can run faster…" began Alan.

"What? ALL Earth men can run faster than ALL Earth women?" asked Lok.

"No, no. Some men can run faster than some women."

"And how is that helpful to be a ruler?" asked Bok, genuinely interested.

"Well," explained Alan. "If you needed to get somewhere quickly, for example…"

"But you have cars and bikes and trains and boats and planes."

"Yes, well, forget the running part. That might not be so important these days. But men are taller than women," said Alan.

The aliens looked at Alan's short, squat body and before they could open their mouths, Alan quickly added, "Not ALL men, but some men are taller than some women."

"And how is that useful?" asked Mok, mystified.

"Well…" stammered Alan, "I suppose if you wanted to reach something from a high shelf…"

"Like a jar?" suggested Lok.

"Yes, a jar! Exactly! And then perhaps that jar needed to be opened…" said Alan excitedly.

"Yes, and then maybe lots of jars needed reaching and opening and putting in a suitcase and then carrying somewhere – then a man could do that?" suggested Bok.

"Yes! Yes! You see? Now you're getting it! That's **EXACTLY** the kind of thing a man could do better than a woman," said Alan triumphantly. "Some men," he added quietly.

"And how often do your SUPREME LEADERS have to reach for jars and open them and transport them in suitcases – as part of their daily duties?" asked Mok.

"Not that often," admitted Alan. "But if some sort of jar situation, or indeed jar crisis, should ever arise," said Alan, "then men would be able to deal with it very easily. Some of them."

"That is most fascinating," said Bok, trying not to laugh again. "We shall be sure to pass this on to the SUPREME LEADER once we get home."

At that moment, Alan's wife Pam came out, looking for Alan.

"Alan!" she shouted crossly over the fence. "I can't find my selfie stick anywhere! Did you use it as a lever in your stupid rocket?"

"**THE SUPREME LEADER!**" gasped all the aliens, bowing deeply to Pam.

"**Aaaaaaaaaaaaaa aaaaaaaaaaaaaaaaa aaaaarrrrrrggggghh!**"
she said much louder.

"**Aaaaaaaaaaaaaaaaaaaa aaaaaaaaaaaaaaaaaaaaaa aaaaarrrrrrggggghh!**" she said
croakily.

"**Arrrrrrrrgggggggggggggggggggghhhhhhhhh!**"
she said very quietly indeed because by now
she was losing her voice.

"An alien invasion!" she observed in a
screamy whisper.

"SUPREME LEADER, most wise woman,
most important woman, most wonderful
woman," said Bok. "It is an honour to meet
you."

"Charmed, I'm sure," said Pam.

"We need to take your husband Alan away. To Mars," explained Mok.

"OK. Fine," said Pam.

"Before you say no, let us explain," continued Mok. "He crashed his rocket into the palace of our Supreme Leader and damaged it and therefore he must come and fix it."

"Yes, yes, fine," said Pam. "Take as long as you like."

"Perhaps you would care to come too?" asked Lok.

"No, I'm a bit busy," said Pam. "I might miss an episode of one of my reality TV programmes that I like to watch."

"That is a great shame. The SUPREME LEADER OF MARS has always wanted to meet the SUPREME LEADER OF EARTH..."

"Oh well. Never mind," said Pam.

"And lavish her with gifts. Gifts upon gifts upon gifts," said Bok. "Many plentiful gifts. Gifts beyond your wildest imagination."

"On the other hand," said Pam. "Maybe I could come after all. I'll get my bag."

"Make sure it is a very big bag," said Mok, "for I don't know if we mentioned it, but there will be many, many gifts."

"Many, many gifts," repeated Lok.

Pam scurried off excitedly.

Alan turned to the aliens. "If I have to go back to Mars to fix your palace, then I must take my robot."

"You have a robot?" asked Bok, looking impressed.

"Oh yes," said Alan smugly. "He is called Mark III and I built him to do my every bidding. Watch."

Alan called over the fence to Mark III who was lying on a sun lounger, having a nap.

"Mark III? Mark III? Come here."

Mark III didn't move.

"Watch this," said Alan. "I can ask him any question and he knows the answer."

Alan turned grandly to his robot.

"How far away is Mars?" he said.

There was no reply.

"Mark III? How far is Mars?"

"I don't know. Leave me alone," said Mark III.

"Don't be silly, of course you know," said Alan, looking embarrassed.

"Why are you always picking on me?" moaned Mark III.

"I'm not picking on you," said Alan, "I'm just saying, how far is Mars?"

"I don't know," grumbled Mark III. "What's Mars?"

"What's Mars? What's Mars? I've spent

fourteen years uploading information to you and you ask me what Mars is? Why do I bother?" yelped Alan, hopping from foot to foot with irritation.

"I dunno," said Mark III with a shrug.

Alan climbed over the fence and walked up to Mark III and whispered to him. "You know very well that Mars is a planet. Stop embarrassing me in front of everyone. Remember what I said earlier about behaving more like a sophisticated high-tech robot? Well, start doing it or there will be no pocket money."

Mark III tutted and sighed.

"Now," said Alan loudly. "How far is Mars?"

"I have no results for 'How far is Mars'," said Mark III. "However, I have seven thousand eight hundred and ninety-six results for your previous question, 'How do you treat an itchy bottom?'"

"I did NOT ask about an itchy bottom," said Alan, blushing furiously.

"Yes, you did," said Mark III. "On July 31st at 2.37 pm," he added proudly.

"All right, all right. Forget about itchy bottoms," said Alan. "Just get on the spaceship."

"I can't do that, because I need upgrading," explained Mark III.

"Again? I just upgraded you last week!"

"Well, now I need upgrading again," said Mark III.

"Will it cost money?" asked Alan.

"Yes. But all my friends have been upgraded," said Mark III.

"Fine, fine," said Alan sighing.

Wilf helped Alan climb back over the fence and Mark III slouched along behind them. Alan asked Wilf if he would look after Kevin Phillips while he was gone. Wilf said he would, and was just listening to Alan run through a complicated list of Kevin's likes and dislikes and dietary requirements and funny little foibles, when Pam came staggering back through the garden carrying eighteen empty suitcases.

"Excellent! We are ready to go," said Bok. "And I trust you have gifts for the SUPREME LEADER to give in return?"

"Er…well, no. Not exactly," admitted Pam. "I don't really know what she likes."

"What about a book token?" said Wilf. "That's always a good present."

"Books are rubbish," said Pam. "Who needs books?"

"Then perhaps some of your Earth clothes would amuse her?" suggested Mok.

"No, no – I need all my clothes," said Pam.

"Or maybe some of your jewellery?" suggested Lok.

"No, no, I DEFINITELY need that," said Pam hurriedly. "I know! Does she have a small human with pingy ears or a tiny odorous creature or a small furry thing with four legs?"

"I don't believe she has any of those things," said Bok.

"Great. She can have them then," said Pam, pointing to Wilf, Dot and Kevin Phillips.

And so, to Wilf's horror, he found himself and Dot and Kevin being plonked on the spaceship.

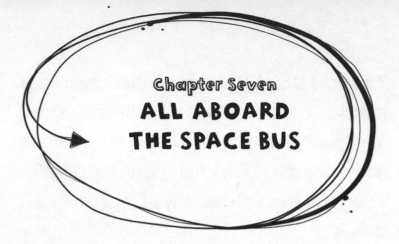

Chapter Seven
ALL ABOARD
THE SPACE BUS

Well, I don't know how often you've taken off into space in an alien spaceship, but as you will probably know, it's quite lurchy. And also your face goes all stretchy in a floopy way. And if you've got pingy ears they ping like they've never pinged before.

Wilf was scared and went rather pale and quiet while Dot bounced up and down on her seat shouting, "Wheeeeeeeeeeeeeee! Bus!"

"It's not a bus, Dot," said Wilf. "It's an alien spaceship."

"Actually, it is a bus," said Bok. "It's a Space Bus. We will be going home to Mars via Venus and Mercury."

Wilf looked out of his porthole and saw Earth getting smaller and smaller. He didn't like going away from home. Even to Granny's house, which was only about an hour's drive. And Mars was a lot further than that. He suddenly felt very small. And very lonely.

Just then, a tiny green hand reached for his hand. It was Lok.

"I don't like going away either," said Lok. "They have different rocks. And a different numbers of moons."

"Yes, and different pillows," said Wilf.

"It makes my tummy feel all churny," said Lok.

"Yes, and my eyebrows feel all runkly," said Wilf.

"I don't have eyebrows," said Lok. "But I bet if I did, they would be very runkly right now." He smiled and squeezed Wilf's hand.

After several million miles, the Space Bus stopped at a space bus stop on Venus. A very slurpy-looking alien slurped on, with eyes on

stalks and suckers on the end of his legs and arms.

"Vavoovoo!" said Lok excitedly, clapping his hands.

"Hello!" said Vavoovoo. "I was hoping I'd see you. Guess what? I'm going on holiday to Marszzzzzzzz…"

Vavoovoo stopped talking. His eyes began to close and his head fell forward – but just as his chin reached his chest, his eyes opened again and his head jerked upwards. "Huh? Wha? What's happening?"

"You were telling us about your holiday," prompted Wilf helpfully.

"Oh yes," said Vavoovoo. "I really need a holiday because I'm so..." Before Vavoovoo could finish his sentence, he did the most enormous

yaaaaaaaaaawn.

He smacked his lips. "What was I saying?"

"That you need a holiday..." said Wilf.

"Oh yes. I need a holiday because I'm so..." But before Vavoovoo could finish his sentence again, he started snoring.

Every time he breathed in, his trumpet-shaped nose trumpeted. And every time he breathed out, his big rubbery blue lips blew a very long raspberry.

Dot giggled.

Vavoovoo woke up. "Where was I?"

"You were saying you need a holiday," said Wilf again.

"Yes. Because I'm so… What's the word? Sorry, my head's all fuzzy and woozy and I can't remember anything. What's that word when you feel sleepy and you need a rest?"

"TIRED! TIRED TIRED TIRED!! THE WORD IS TIRED! YOU ARE TIRED! AND NOW I AM TIRED. TIRED OF YOUR SNORING AND YOUR NODDING OFF AND YOUR TRUMPETING AND YOUR NOT FINISHING YOUR SENTENCE. TIRED TIRED TIRED," said Alan, a little unreasonably.

"Sorry," said Vavoovoo. "The problem is, on Venus, one day is the equivalent of 116 of your Earth days."

"Wow!" said Wilf. "That must be exhausting!"

"It is," said Vavoovoo. "It means my Maths lesson lasts almost five days. And my homework takes nearly a fortnight."

"That's awful!" said Wilf.

"There are some good things," said Vavoovoo. "Lunch goes on for three days. And sometimes I get to play my computer game for ten days in a row."

"I bet your thumbs are tired after that," said Wilf.

"Everything is tired," agreed Vavoovoo. "That's why I'm going on holiday to Mars. Their days are almost the same as your days."

"Why don't you have a holiday on Earth? It's very nice there," said Wilf, looking wistfully out of his porthole again. Earth was about the size of a kiwi fruit now.

"Yes, it does look lovely," said Vavoovoo. "But the people are dreadful."

Wilf wandered over to Alan, wondering as he wandered.

"How long will it take you to mend the SUPREME LEADER'S palace?" asked Wilf. 'Because the thing is, I don't like being away from home. Because of the pillows."

"It won't take any time at all," said Alan.

"Oh goody," said Wilf.

"Because I'm not going to mend it. I sent off for an enormous **Laser Zappy Thing** and I'm going to put that on the roof of the palace and then I'm going to declare myself the **SUPREME LEADER OF THE UNIVERSE** and if anybody disagrees I will **destroy the entire Universe!** "

Wilf went all hot and cold and he felt sick but just in his ears. He wobbled back to his seat and held Lok's hand again. He sucked a travel lozenge but it didn't stop him feeling sick because he didn't have travel sickness – he had worrying-about-the-Universe-ending sickness. And there wasn't a lozenge for that.

A few million miles later the Space Bus stopped at a space bus stop on Mercury. This time a big alien with lots of pointy ears bounced on to the bus.

"Memoo!" said Lok and Vavoovoo together.

"Hello, everyone. Hello, Vavoovoo. What are you doing here?" said Memoo.

"I'm going on holiday to Mars," said Vavoovoo.

"Me too!" said Memoo.

"Why are you going to Mars?" asked Wilf.

"The weather. It's so hot on Mercury," said Memoo, fanning himself with his one enormous flipper.

"How hot?" asked Wilf.

"Today? 427 degrees," said Memoo. "And I am not good in the heat."

As he spoke, a dark patch appeared on his ear.

"Um, excuse me," said Wilf, "but you have a little something. On your ear."

"Which ear?" asked Memoo.

"The third one from the left," said Wilf.

"It's always happening," sighed Memoo, flapping his big flipper harder. As he did so, a little wisp of smoke rose from his ear.

"And now it's...um...smoking," said Wilf anxiously. "And this is a NO SMOKING Space Bus."

"Oh dear, oh dear. Don't you hate it when your ears burst into flames?" said Memoo.

"Well, it's never actually happened to me,"

admitted Wilf, "but I imagine it's awfully inconvenient."

Despite Memoo's flapping flipper, another two ears started smoking.

"Oh dear. Now more of your ears are on fire…"

Memoo flapped his flipper as flippily flappily as he could but soon all eight of his ears were smoking.

"Alan!" yelped Wilf. "Pam! Do something!"

"He's right, we should do something," said Pam. She reached into her bag and brought out two long sticks. She stuck a marshmallow on the end of each stick and gave one to Alan. Then they both began toasting marshmallows on Memoo's flaming ears! And if that isn't the most EVIL thing anybody has EVER done, I don't know what is.

"Dot!" cried Wilf. "What should we do?"

"Happy Birthday to you..." sang Dot. "Happy Birthday to you..."

"No, Dot. Those are not birthday candles, those are his ears. And his head is not a cake. It is his head," explained Wilf.

"Happy Birthday, dear Memoo," sang Dot.

"Maybe if we smothered the fires with your blanky…" suggested Wilf.

"Happy Birthday to yooooouuuuuuuuuuuu," sang Dot.

Wilf grabbed Dot's blanky and threw it over Memoo's head. Almost immediately, Memoo's ears went out.

"Thank you!" cried Memoo.

"Peepo!" shouted Dot, peeping through her blanky, which now had eight singed holes in it.

"It is going to be so much better when I get to Mars," said Memoo.

"How hot is it on Mars?" asked Wilf.

"About 20 degrees."

"That's about the same as where I live on Earth," said Wilf. "Why don't you go there?"

"Yes, the temperatures are very lovely on Earth," agreed Memoo. "But the people are AWFUL. No offence."

"Some taken," said Wilf. "I mean, I think I'm quite nice," said Wilf, "and Dot is nice. If a little smelly."

"And Alan and Pam?" asked Memoo.

"They…" said Wilf.

"Yes?" said Memoo.

"They, well, they…live next door…" said Wilf tactfully.

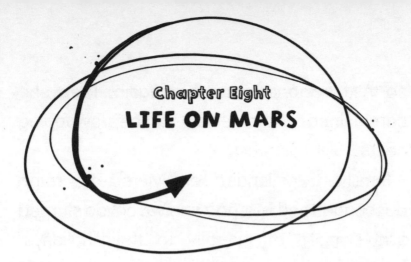

Chapter Eight
LIFE ON MARS

It felt like an awfully long way to Mars. Partly because it is an awfully long way. And partly because the whole way there, Pam was complaining.

First she complained that she didn't have a window seat – so Wilf swapped with her. Then she complained that the driver wasn't taking the best route. Then she complained that she didn't have a seat near the aisle –

so Wilf swapped with her again. Then she complained that she had to keep swapping seats.

Finally, they landed on Mars. The ramp descended and Memoo and Vavoovoo slurped and skipped off happily to their holidays. Pam gathered her eighteen suitcases and complained that they might not be big enough for all her presents.

"Come on, Mark III," said Alan, tripping over Kevin Phillips, who was bravely barking at all the aliens while hiding behind Alan's legs.

"Get off the Space Bus and help me carry my Big Laser...I mean, my luggage."

"I can't," said Mark III.

"Why not?" asked Alan.

"I'm tired," said Mark III.

"You've been asleep the whole way here! You can't be tired!" fumed Alan.

Mark III tutted. "Nobody understands me," he said.

"Are you or are you not going to help me carry my luggage?" said Alan snippily.

"I am not," said Mark III.

"Why not?" asked Alan.

"Because that last upgrade wasn't compatible."

"**Wasn't compatible with what?**"

"I don't know," said Mark III. "It just wasn't."

"**Mark III. Get out of the Space Bus this instant,**" said Alan.

"Can you give me a lift to my friend's house?" asked Mark III.

"**No, I cannot! We're a gabillion miles away on Mars. Now do as I say and get out of the Space Bus!**" fumed Alan.

"Unsubscribe," said Mark III.

"**I'm not an email, I'm a human being!**" said Alan angrily.

"Unsubscribe," said Mark III again.

"**You can't unsubscribe from me. I made you!**" fumed Alan.

"Unsubscribe," said Mark III.

"**Stop saying unsubscribe. I am talking to you and you can't stop me doing that!**"

"People who were interested in me getting out of the Space Bus, also bought itchy bottom cream," said Mark III.

"**Stop talking about my itchy bottom!**" shrieked Alan, and he picked up his enormously long laser-gun-shaped suitcase and wheeled it down the ramp.

Wilf and Dot shuffled tentatively to the top of the ramp and looked out at the strange Martian terrain.

I expect you want to know what Mars looked like. Typical. Nobody warned me that this whole writing thing would involve so much describing things and so much thinking of words. You'll have to use your imagination. It was probably pretty grimlingtons.

"It's beautiful!" gasped Wilf.

(Hmm. Well I reckon it's just full of dusty old rocks.)

"All those beautiful rocks!" added Wilf.

(I bet the whole place was just flat and empty.)

"So many mountains and volcanoes and craters!" said Wilf. (But I bet the sky was just empty and black.)

"Look at those beautiful clouds!" gasped Wilf.

"Moon!" said Dot. "More moon!"

Wilf gazed up at the two moons above them.

"Hurry!" said Bok. "We must get you to the SUPREME LEADER's palace before the children come out of school."

"Why?" asked Wilf.

"Because we do not want them to see you.

It would scare them," explained Mok. "So it is probably best if we fly there. As quickly as possible."

And with that, he shot up into the air.

"Um, the thing is, we can't fly," Wilf shouted after him.

"What are those things at the bottom of your body?" asked Lok. "Aren't they jet thrusters?"

"Um, no. They're legs," said Wilf.

"So how do you get around?" asked Bok.

"We walk!" said Wilf.

"Wow, you really are far down the evolutionary scale," said Mok. "You haven't moved on since the cavemen," he added.

"How rude!" complained Pam. "I will NOT be giving this planet a good review on TripAdvisor."

While Wilf and Dot padded along, looking at the scenery in awed silence, Pam and Alan followed, moaning and carping and grumping and peeving and tripping over Kevin all the way. Mark III slouched and grouched along behind them.

Alan and Pam complained that the street signs were not in English. They complained that Mars didn't have any of their favourite shops or restaurants.

They complained that the red-coloured dust clashed with Pam's pink top.

They complained that the aliens had too many eyes. And too many elbows. And that they were green. Pam didn't like the colour green. She once had a bathroom that was green and she'd never liked it since.

Finally, they all arrived at the SUPREME LEADER's palace. It was humungous, with towers and domes and brightly coloured flags. In front of it was an enormous courtyard with one magnificent tower in the middle. At least, it would have been magnificent if it hadn't been all on the **WONK** because Alan had crashed into it.

"It was the palace's fault!" grumped Alan. "It didn't move out of the way!"

"The SUPREME LEADER is waiting for you," Bok said, ushering the humans to a large door.

"Your Supremeness," said Bok. "The humans are here. The SUPREME LEADER OF EARTH and her husband. And they have gifts for you. Very unusual gifts," he added, pushing Wilf and Dot and Kevin Phillips forward.

"Oh good!" said the SUPREME LEADER. "I'm starving! Let's turn the smallest one into a soup."

Chapter Nine
WILF SOUP

"Meep!" meeped Wilf.

Getting turned into soup was on his latest list of things he was scared of.

But Wilf realized there was something worse than being turned into a soup. And that was watching Dot get turned into a soup.

Wilf was scarified. He felt all trembly and wibbly. His ears went all hot and his eyes went all fuzzy and his knees wanted to bend the wrong way.

He wanted to run and hide and knit and whistle and be a boy for ever, and not someone who has to watch his sister turned into a liquid lunch.

Wilf reached for his **HOW TO STOP WORRYING LEAFLET**. **Number Five** said –

5) It can make you feel better if you list all your achievements.

Right. Achievements. Wilf had a think.

Well, I nearly got my **BEGINNERS SWIMMING CERTIFICATE** but then I didn't because I was too scared of putting my face under water.

And I very nearly got my **LEVEL ONE RECORDER CERTIFICATE** but then I didn't because I was so nervous I couldn't breathe and breathing is

important for playing the recorder.

Then at school my teacher said I was a very good dancer and I would do very well at ballet but I was worried about what everyone would think of me if I did ballet so I didn't do it.

Then my cousin joined the Scouts and got these great badges and I wanted to join and get great badges but I was too scared to join because I didn't want to go camping because I don't like being away from home or sleeping in tents and so I didn't join and I didn't get any badges.

Wilf sighed. His whole life had been a long list of things he didn't do or he didn't achieve because he was scared or worried or nervous. And that in turn was making him scared and worried and nervous that he would never do **ANYTHING**. This had to stop!

Wilf had a great big old worry and then a great big old think and then he thought so hard his brain got a puncture and then he had an idea!

The SUPREME LEADER wanted soup. But he didn't want Dot to become soup. So there was only one thing for it. He had to be turned into a soup instead of Dot.

He grabbed his packed lunch from his rucksack and he stepped forward.

"Hello, Mrs SUPREME LEADER. I think I would make a very delicious soup. You could poach me or caramelize me or batter me or even fricassee me. Or maybe julienne me – that means slice me into thin strips. Or sauté me. And then look," he said, grabbing his cheese sandwich, "you could sprinkle cheese on me. Or maybe add some croutons," he said, crumbling some bread and cheese on to his head.

The SUPREME LEADER looked at Wilf. "Why would I want to eat you?" she asked, sounding confused.

"Er. Because you're hungry?" said Wilf.

"But you look very chewy," said the SUPREME LEADER. "And bony," she added. "Also, I only eat rocks."

"But you said you wanted to eat your gifts," said Wilf. "And we're your gifts."

"Oh! I assumed the SUPREME LEADER OF EARTH had brought me rocks. I love rocks," said the SUPREME LEADER.

"So, you're not going to turn Dot into soup?" asked Wilf.

"I'd rather not," said the SUPREME LEADER, looking at Dot nervously. "I think I might catch something. Also, it doesn't seem like a very friendly thing to do."

"That's wonderful news!" beamed Wilf.

"Where are my gifts?" interrupted Pam huffily. "I've been here for ages now and I haven't got a gift yet."

"Of course!" said the SUPREME LEADER. "They are here. Eighteen of the most fabulous gifts," she said, stepping aside and revealing a pile of rocks. "You can eat them now or save them for later," said the SUPREME LEADER. "They get better with age."

"But they're rocks," said Pam, disappointed.

"Yes!" said the SUPREME LEADER happily. "Some of our **BEST** rocks."

"I thought you were going to give me jewels and money and Argos vouchers and more jewels," whined Pam.

"Oh no. I would never insult you with such pointless gifts," said the SUPREME LEADER.

"I don't mind being insulted with jewellery," said Pam.

"No, no. I wouldn't dream of it. You deserve the best. You deserve rocks."

"But what can I do with a rock?" asked Pam.

"What can't you do with a rock?" said the SUPREME LEADER. "You can eat them or look at them or play with them or hold them. They are a work of art. A piece of history. A living sculpture. All rolled into one."

"I love rocks," said Wilf. "I have an extensive pebble collection at home."

"You see?" said the SUPREME LEADER, turning to Pam.

"OK," said Pam. "But if I don't like them, can I just get my money back?"

"Of course!" said the SUPREME LEADER.

"Great!" said Pam.

"Although, I probably should tell you," said the SUPREME LEADER, "that on Mars, our money is rocks."

"I wish I'd never come!" stropped Pam. "I don't like my gifts and I don't like your planet!"

"I am sorry to hear that," said the SUPREME LEADER. "What is it you don't like?"

"Everything," said Pam. "It's all just too... different."

"I see," said the SUPREME LEADER. "Your planet must be a wonderful place. Tell me about it."

"We can do better than that," said Alan. "Mark III?" he called.

"What now?" huffed Mark III.

"Please show a video of what life is like on Earth," said Alan.

"Why me?" sulked Mark III. "Why can't someone else do it?"

"Because you're my robot and I've asked you to," said Alan evenly.

"This is SO unfair!" sighed Mark III.

"I do a lot of things for you," said Alan, "so can you please do this one thing for me."

"I'll do it later," said Mark III.

"No. I'd like you to do it now please," said Alan.

Alan waited. Nothing happened.

"Mark III?" repeated Alan.

No response.

"Mark III! Show a video of life on Earth right now!" snapped Alan.

"I'm buffering," said Mark III.

"Buffering? Why are you buffering? What's buffering?"

"It's when you want to watch something and it's slow to play," explained Mark III.

"Well, stop it!" squeaked Alan. **"Stop buffering this instant!"**

Mark III continued to buffer.

"Just fix the stupid blooming palace," Pam said to Alan. "And then we can get out of this awful place and go home." She stomped off back to the Space Bus to wait for him.

Chapter Ten
ALAN,
THE SUPREME LEADER
OF THE UNIVERSE

"So, Alan," said the SUPREME LEADER. "Are you going to fix my palace?"

"Oh, I'm going to fix it all right," said Alan, menacingly.

"Wonderful," said the SUPREME LEADER. "And is there anything you'd like to say to me?"

"You're welcome," said Alan, hoity-toitily.

"I think you're meant to say sorry," Wilf whispered to Alan.

"I can't!" Alan whispered back. "I've never apologized to anyone in my life. I don't know how."

"Just repeat after me," said Wilf. "I'm sorry."

"I'm sorry?" said Alan.

"No, that sounded like you hadn't heard what I'd said," said Wilf. "Try again. I'm sorry."

"I'm sorry," said Alan.

"Well, that time you sounded sarcastic," said Wilf.

"I'm sorrrrrrrrrrrry," said Alan.

"OK, this isn't working," said Wilf. "You just sound sulky and angry."

"Because I am sulky and angry!" said Alan, sulkily and angrily.

"I think the problem is that you don't feel sorry," said Wilf.

"Exactly!" said Alan. "Because it wasn't

my fault. I was trying to park and the palace wouldn't move out of the way."

"Perhaps," said the SUPREME LEADER, "I should just let you go home. I will mend the palace myself."

"That sounds like a jolly good idea," said Wilf enthusiastically.

"No, no, I'm going to mend your palace!" insisted Alan, sounding a little panicked.

"It's very kind of you, but your wife, the SUPREME LEADER, wants to go home so…"

"No, I INSIST on mending the palace. I've got it all planned out. I've brought the big laser…er, tools and everything," said Alan, pointing at his big laser-gun-shaped suitcase.

"Well, how about instead of mending the palace, you build a hospital or a school?" asked the SUPREME LEADER.

"Building hospitals and schools is boring and stupid, and that is exactly why women shouldn't be in charge," said Alan huffily.

"Really?" said the SUPREME LEADER, looking amused.

"Yes, REALLY," said Alan. "And one day there will be a man not just in charge of Mars but in charge of the **whole Universe.**"

"I'm not sure that's a good idea," said the SUPREME LEADER.

"Of course it's a good idea. Didn't your people tell you about the whole jar and suitcase thing?" asked Alan.

"Yes, they did mention that..." said the SUPREME LEADER, chuckling to herself.

"Very well, I will let you get on with your task."

"Good," said Alan. "The sooner I attach the **Big Laser Zappy** – I mean the tower to the roof of the palace – the better."

And off he went, laughing an evil laugh.

Chapter Eleven
PLANET PET DAY

Wilf watched Alan hauling his big laser-gun-shaped suitcase down the steps of the palace. He suddenly felt very sick. But just in his neck. And his knees wanted to bend the wrong way. And his eyes felt all hot.

"Excuse me, SUPREME LEADER?" said Wilf.

"Please, call me Su," said the SUPREME LEADER.

"Um, Su, you see, the thing is, Alan is the baddest man in the whole wide world and I think he is going to do something very bad indeed."

"Nonsense," said Su. "He seems lovely."

"Well, don't let him hear you say that," said Wilf. "He wouldn't like it at all. But I think you're right – deep down he is lovely – but he doesn't believe that, so he keeps wanting to prove that he's bad. And he's going to do a bad thing."

"Oh, I'm sure he's harmless enough," said Su. "He insisted on mending the palace even when I tried to let him off!"

"Yes," said Wilf anxiously. "That's what worries me."

"Now if you'll excuse me, I must go," said Su. "We have a big festival today on Mars.

It's **PLANET PET DAY**. Everyone on Mars brings their pets to the palace courtyard and the owners and their pets have a commitment ceremony where they promise to look after each other for the next year."

"That sounds like a wonderful idea!" said Wilf. "My pet is my best friend, Stuart. He is a woodlouse. We would really like to be part of your ceremony."

"Then you shall," said Su. "I will see you in the palace courtyard later." She blobbed out of the room.

There was just one problem. If Alan wasn't stopped, there would be no ceremony. In fact, there would be no courtyard, no palace, no aliens and no pets. No Wilf, no Dot, no Stuart. No you, no me.

Wait! What? No me? That

would be awful. Wilf has to do something!

"Bok?" called Wilf.

"Bok," replied Dot helpfully.

But Bok was nowhere to be seen.

"Mok?" called Wilf.

"Mok," replied Dot helpfully.

But Mok was nowhere to be seen either.

"Lok?" called Wilf.

"He's not here," said Lok. "He's somewhere else completely. He's definitely not hiding under the table."

Wilf looked under the table. "There you are!" he said.

"How did you know I was here?" asked Lok, amazed.

"Just a hunch," said Wilf. "Now listen, Lok, you need to take me to the big tower in the middle of the palace courtyard as quickly as possible. Alan is there and he is planning something terrible."

"But I can't!" wailed Lok. "Didn't you hear what the SUPREME LEADER said? It's **PLANET PET DAY**! And I'm terrified of pets! I'm worried they might bite me!" Lok trembled at the very thought. "When I think about them, I feel sick. But just in my neck. And my knees want to bend the wrong way. And my eyes feel all hot."

"I know exactly how you feel!" said Wilf. "But I can help. I have a leaflet!"

Wilf showed it to Lok.

Number 6 said – *It can help to pretend*

you are blowing up a balloon with three deep breaths.

"Let's try that one," said Wilf.

Together, he and Lok took a big deep breath and then Wilf blewwwwwwwwwwwwwwwwwwwww out his breath slowly. Then they took another big deep breath and Wilf blewwwwwwwwwwwwwwwwwww into the imaginary balloon. Then they took another big deep breath and Wilf was about to blowwwwwwwwwwwww when he noticed Lok floating up past him to the ceiling.

"Don't forget to breathe out!" cried Wilf.

Lok looked down anxiously as he floated higher and higher.

"Breathe out!" repeated Wilf.

Lok took another big deep breath in. He floated even higher.

"**Not in! Out!**" called Wilf.

"Hokey cokey," agreed Dot.

Lok took another big deep breath in. He floated even higher.

"Oh no!" cried Wilf. "Dot! Do something!"

Dot looked very serious. She frowned. And then she let out an extremely stinky blow off.

"Pewwwwwwwwwww!" said Lok, breathing out and flapping the air away from his face with his hands. As he did so, he stopped floating

and tumbled back down, landing in Wilf's arms.

"OK, well, that didn't help much," admitted Wilf. "Let's look at Number 7."

Number 7 said – *A stress ball can help in stressful situations.*

"That's actually true," said Wilf, "and I happen to have one with me."

Wilf got out his yellow stress ball and handed it to Lok. Lok popped it in his mouth and swallowed.

"It's not working," said Lok.

"Yes, well, you're not meant to eat it, you're meant to squeeze it! Here, I've got another one," said Wilf, handing it to Lok.

Lok started squeezing.

"Is it working?" asked Wilf.

"No!" said Lok. "It's making me feel worse!"

"Why?" asked Wilf.

"Because I worry I'm going to break it and then you won't like me any more and I won't know where to get you another one and I worry I might squeeze it so hard it flies out of my hand and hits someone on the head or breaks a window or falls in someone's soup or trips someone over or…"

"OK, stop stop!" said Wilf. "The stress ball is just making you stressed. We'll have to think of something else."

Wilf thought and thought and he thought so hard his brain nearly ran out of batteries and then he had an idea.

"What do pets on Mars eat?" asked Wilf.

"If they're big they eat pebbles. If they're smaller, they eat gravel and if they're tiny, they eat sand."

"Right," said Wilf, "we'll take plenty of their favourite food so that they want to eat that instead of you."

Wilf and Lok and Dot filled their pockets (and nappy) with pebbles and gravel and sand.

"And one other thing," said Wilf. "I used to be scared of dogs and cats and birds and pretty much all pets – until I got a pet, Stuart. And he made me realize that pets can be nice. So as a special treat, you can borrow Stuart and have him as your pet."

And with that, Wilf opened his top pocket. But before he could fish Stuart out, Stuart came floating up past them. Because there is less gravity on Mars, Stuart wasn't heavy enough to stay on Wilf's hand. So Wilf got a little piece of cotton and tied it round Stuart, turning Stuart into a little tiny woodlouse-shaped balloon.

Wilf handed the Stuart balloon over to Lok.

"Right. Let's go and save the Universe!" said Wilf.

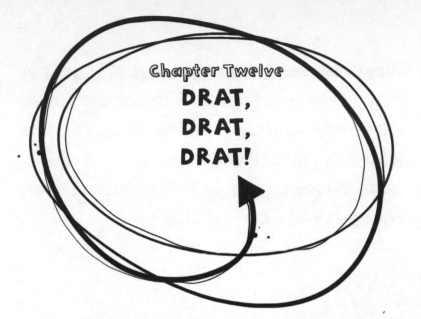

Chapter Twelve

DRAT, DRAT, DRAT!

And so Wilf and Dot and Lok and Stuart set off across the palace courtyard towards the tower. As they walked, they passed aliens with their pets. They were all sorts of extraordinary colours and all sorts of extraordinary shapes with feathers and scales and fur and tails and beaks and hooves – it was an incredible sight.

Lok walked bravely through the crowds, holding Wilf's hand with one hand and his

Stuart balloon in the other. Not a single pet tried to bite Lok, but LOTS of aliens stopped and complimented Lok on his pet. Lok's smile got bigger and bigger.

"Are these ALL your pets?" asked one alien, looking at Wilf, Dot and Stuart.

"Yes, we are," said Wilf.

"You have the BEST pets!" said the alien.

Lok giggled, Wilf beamed and Dot was so excited, she bit Lok.

"Ouch!" said Lok.

"I'm so sorry," said Wilf. "She does that when she's excited. But that just shows that sometimes, when something you're worried about actually happens, it's not as bad as you thought it might be."

"That's very true," said Lok, patting Dot on the head and then wiping his hand because even though he was sticky and slimy, Dot's head was much stickier and slimier.

Finally, Wilf and Dot and Lok and Stuart saw the bottom of the great tower ahead of them.

And then they saw Bok strapping one jet pack on to Alan and another on to Mark III and a third on to Kevin Phillips. And before Wilf could stop him, the three of them had zoomed up into the air, carrying Alan's large laser-gun-shaped suitcase.

"**Where has he gone?**" cried Wilf.

"To mend the tower of course," said Bok. "Are you going to help him?"

"Um. Something like that," said Wilf. "Could we have a jet pack too?"

"Of course!" said Bok. And he strapped Wilf into a jet pack, with Dot tucked into a little baby seat at the front.

"The green button means..." started Bok, but before he could finish, Wilf had rocketed up into the air and could only hear the words "**Try not to press it too hard!**" from a long way away.

"What does the red button do?"

shouted Wilf.

The red button means..." started Bok.

"Down" he said, his voice getting louder and louder as Wilf plummeted to the ground.

"You'll get the hang of it," said Bok. "Or possibly not," he added, as Wilf went badoinging round and round.

"**I hope so,**" said Wilf, dizzily. And up he shot again.

He could see Alan in the distance, heading for the broken tower.

"**I wonder which one means forwards?**" said Wilf to Dot. "**Probably yelloooooooooooooow,**" he said, hurtling backwards at top speed until –

THWACK

– he slammed into another tower of the Supreme Palace, leaving a Wilf-shaped dent in it.

"Oops," said Wilf.

"Boo," said Dot.

"OK," said Wilf. "Let's try blue."

He pressed blue and they zoomed forward, whizzing through the starry sky.

Suddenly, Lok appeared next to him, jetting along on his little thrusty legs.

"You helped me," said Lok, "so now I'm going to help you."

"Are you sure?" said Wilf.

"Yes," said Lok. "Stuart is making me feel brave."

"He makes me feel brave, too!" said Wilf.

Wilf and Dot and Lok and Stuart headed towards Alan and had almost caught up with him, when suddenly dozens and dozens of tiny aliens crossed their path, jet thrusting home from school on their jet thrusty legs.

"**Aaargh! Aliens!**" screamed the tiny aliens.

"I knew aliens existed!" said one tiny alien, "but everyone said I was mad!"

"But you are aliens!" said Wilf.

"**No, we live here — YOU are aliens!**" squealed the aliens.

"Don't panic," said Wilf. "We come in peace. Well, actually, most of us come in peace – one of us came to destroy the Universe. So on second thoughts – **PANIC!**"

The tiny aliens went whizzing off in all directions, panicking. Wilf looked around, but Alan was nowhere to be seen. Where had he gone with his **Laser Zapper Thingy**?

At that moment, a huge laser zapper swung round from the other side of the tower, hitting Wilf on the side.

"Ooooffff!" said Wilf.

"Sorry," said Alan. "And when I say sorry, I mean I'm sorry I didn't hit you harder!"

And with that, Alan leaned over and pulled the jet pack off Wilf's back. Wilf and Dot started falling to the ground!

Fally fall.

Fally fall.

Fally fall.

(It was a long way down.)

Fally fall.

Fally fall.

Fally fall.

(Also, there's less gravity on Mars so it takes longer.)

Fally fall.

Fally fall.

(But it doesn't make it any less scary.)

"**Heeeeeeeeelp!**" cried Wilf.

"I'm coming!" said Lok.

"**Heeeeeeeeelp!**" Wilf cried again.

"Wait for me!" said Lok.

"And in case I haven't mentioned it before," said Wilf. "**Help!**"

Wilf scrunched up his eyes waiting for the splat as he hit the ground, but instead there was a floppity flop flip flop noise. He had landed in Memoo's large flippers!

"You caught us!" said Wilf, astonished.

"I heard you cry for help," said Memoo. "That's the good thing about having eight ears. You can hear really well. When your ears

aren't on fire. Which mine aren't any more –
thanks to you."

Memoo set Wilf and Dot on the ground.
"What were you doing up there in the first
place?" asked Memoo.

"It's Alan," said Wilf. "He's up on the tower – and he's going to destroy the Universe. We've got to do something!"

"How can we get up there?" asked Memoo.

"I don't know. I can't fly!" said Wilf.

"Neither can I!" said Memoo. "But maybe Vavoovoo can help." He pointed to the distance where Vavoovoo was slurping towards them on his suckery feet.

"Quick, Vavoovoo, Wilf needs to get up to the tower!" said Memoo.

Lok landed next to them. "I can fly! I'll carry you!" said Lok.

"I'm too big. You take Dot. And Vavoovoo will take me."

With trembling arms, Wilf put Dot onto Lok's back and then climbed onto Vavoovoo's back. Vavoovoo started climbing up the tower, each sucker making a big slurpy sound with every step. No sooner had they climbed a few feet up the tower, than they heard Alan's voice.

"**People of Mars,**" boomed Alan through a loudspeaker. "**I bring you good news!**"

"Ooh! Everybody's going get a free rock!" said the people of Mars excitedly.

"**No. Better than that.**"

"Everybody's going to get TWO free rocks?"

"**No. Even better than that,**" said Alan.

"Everybody's going to be given…"

"**IT'S NOT ABOUT ROCKS!**"

yelled Alan.

"But we like our old SUPREME LEADER," said the people of Mars.

"**Well, you'll like the new one even more.**"

"Impossible!" said the people of Mars.

"**No, it's not impossible,**" said Alan. "**Because it's me!**"

The people of Mars laughed. "No, really, who is it?"

"**It's me,**" repeated Alan.

"No, but really," they said.

"**Me!**" said Alan.

"No, but seriously," they said.

"**It's me!**" he shouted.

"No, but who is it?" they asked.

"**ME ME ME ME ME ME ME ME ME!**" yelled Alan.

"It can't be you, you're a man," said one Martian.

"Maybe he isn't a man," said another. "Maybe he's a lady with a moustache."

"**I am not a lady with a moustache,**" said Alan. "**I am a man. And I am going to be a better SUPREME LEADER than the other one because I am a man.**"

The people of Mars laughed again.

"**No. Wait. Listen. Has anyone told you about how I can undo jars?**" said Alan. "**If Pam loosens them up a bit first.**"

"We don't have jars on Mars," said the people of Mars.

"**All right, all right. I can carry heavy suitcases though,**" said Alan. "**If my back isn't playing up.**"

"We don't have those either," said the people of Mars.

"Ridiculous planet," said Pam crossly, standing by the Space Bus with her arms folded.

"Are you, or are you not, going to let me be SUPREME LEADER of Mars and indeed the whole Universe?" asked Alan.

"We are not," said the people of Mars.

"You don't have to answer straight away..." said Alan.

"We are definitely not," repeated the people of Mars.

"You can think about it for a while if you like..." offered Alan.

"No, thanks!" said the people of Mars. "We've made up our minds."

"Fine," said Alan. **"Well, you may be interested to know that I am the**

baddest, the baddest, the biddly boddly baddest man in the whole wide worlderoony — and now I shall destroy the **ENTIRE UNIVERSE**. And you shall all be zapped. Zippity zoppity zapped. And obliterated into...obliterations. So there."

Meanwhile, unseen by Alan, Wilf and Vavoovoo were slowly slurping up one side of the tower, while Lok, Dot and Stuart jetted up the other side.

"Wouldn't it be more fun," suggested the people of Mars, "if we played some games together, or had a sing-a-long? Or maybe baked a cake?"

"**No!**" shouted Alan. "**It would NOT. It would not be fun AT ALL. What would be most fun is** if I killed everyone in the whole Universe and you were all **dead. Deadity deadity dead.**"

Wilf and Vavoovoo edged closer.

"**Deadity deadity deadity deadingtons.**"

Lok, Dot and Stuart had almost reached the ledge.

"**Deadity doddity doo. A doobery doo.**"

Wilf and Vavoovoo edged closer still.

"**And then I think everyone will agree that I am the biddly boddly baddest man in the whole wide universeroony. So there. The end. Full stop. Nobody can disagree with me. The end. Shut up. I get the last word. The End.**"

Wilf and Vavoovoo hauled themselves up on to the base of the **Laser Zappy Thingy**.

"Hello," said Wilf. "Fancy seeing you up here."

"Oh no you don't," said Alan. "No no no no. Noooooo noooooo noooooo. Not this time. Because all I have to do is power up my **Laser Zappy Thing** and then it's all over."

"OK, well, hang on a minute," said Wilf, reaching for his backpack so that he could get out his **HOW TO STOP WORRYING** leaflet.

"Don't even think about it!" said Alan. And with one kick of his long poky foot, he kicked the backpack out of Wilf's hands. They watched as it slowly floated towards the ground.

Lok reached out his hand and tried to catch the backpack, but he missed and it carried on falling.

Wilf was horrified. What was he going to do now? His leaflet was gone. He didn't have anything to help him. He didn't have a plan. And, most of all, he didn't have time to worry. And there was nothing he would have liked more than to have a big old worry. But he couldn't. It was just Wilf. The future of the

whole Universe depended on him. And even though his eyebrows hurt and his neck was hot and he felt sick (but just in his nose) and his knees were bending the wrong way like billy-o, he had to DO something.

Alan reached for a big **ON** button. Wilf hurled himself towards him. They scuffled and wrestled and scrapped and tussled and tangled.

"Mark III," gasped Alan. "Turn on the **Laser Zappy Thingy!**"

"Okaaaaaaaay," said Mark III. "No need to over-react."

"**I'm not over-reacting! This is an emergency!**" squealed Alan.

"If I do it, can I have extra pocket money?" said Mark III.

"**Yes, yes! Whatever you want! Just do it quickly!**"

"I don't know how to," said Mark III.

"**What do you mean you don't know how to?**" squealed Alan. "**You helped me to build it. You created the password, you made the big ON button, you helped me test it.**"

"I don't remember," shrugged Mark III.

"**But I input that information on your hard drive myself!**" squeaked Alan.

"But you didn't back it up," said Mark III.

"**What?**"

"You didn't back it up," repeated Mark III.

"**So where is it?**" asked Alan.

"Gone," said Mark III.

"**Gone? Gone? How can it be gone? Gone where?**"

Mark III shrugged. "Just gone," he said.

"That can happen," agreed Wilf, sympathetically. And in that instant, he took his eyes off Alan, and Alan reached over and switched the **ON** button **ON**.

There was a tremendous whirring and buzzing and thrumming. A huge timer popped up and started counting down towards the end of the Universe.

"**Oh no!**" screamed Wilf.

"Quick!" said Vavoovoo. "Wilf, you type in

the password to stop it. Lok, you deal with Alan and Mark III and Kevin Phillips."

And with that, Lok reached into his pockets and threw a large pebble at Alan. It missed, but Kevin Phillips gave an excited woof and leapt off the platform to go and retrieve it.

Lok reached into his pockets again and threw all the sand.

"Not the hair! Not the hair!" shouted Alan angrily, trying to brush the sand out of his hair.

Lok reached into his pockets a third time and threw all the gravel he had. It was a direct hit! Alan and Mark III teetered backwards on the edge of the ledge, arms wheeling.

Wilf reached into his pocket and threw the stress ball at Alan. It was enough to knock him off the ledge, taking Mark III with him.

As they tumbled slowly to the ground, Alan shouted, "It's too late, you idiots! It's too late!"

TEN flashed the timer.

"Quick, Dot, think! What's the password?"

"Tractor," suggested Dot.

NINE flashed the timer.

"I know that's your favourite word but I don't think it's Alan's favourite word. Oh what could it be? What could it be?"

EIGHT flashed the timer.

"Doggy woggy woof woof," said Dot.

"Yes! Brilliant idea! Alan loves Kevin. Let's try that."

SEVEN flashed the timer.

Wilf typed '**KEVIN PHILLIPS**' with trembling fingers.

INCORRECT said the control pad.

SIX flashed the timer.

"Oh no! That's not right. Think again, think again! Think of something you know about Alan," said Wilf.

FIVE flashed the timer.

"Itchy bottom," said Dot.

FOUR flashed the timer.

"Well, he won't thank you for saying that," said Wilf. "But let's give it a try."

He typed the words **'ITCHY BOTTOM'** into the control pad.

INCORRECT said the control pad. **ONLY ONE TRY REMAINING**.

"Oh no!" said Wilf. "It's all over!

THREE flashed the timer.

"**The Universe is going to end!**" wailed Wilf. "**I failed. Just like with my swimming and the recorder and ballet and the Scouts.**"

TWO flashed the timer.

"I'm sorry, everyone," said Wilf. "I've blown it. I haven't saved the Universe. **Drat drat drat**. Wait a minute! That must be it! Drat drat drat! That was Alan's password for Mark III and Mark put in the password for the **Laser Zapper Thingy!**"

ONE flashed the timer.

D–R–A–T–D–R–A–T–D–R–A–T he typed.

CORRECT said the control pad!

The **Laser Zapper Thingy** abruptly switched off.

The Universe was saved!

The people of Mars cheered.

Wilf, Dot and Lok cheered.

Memoo and Vavoovoo cheered.

Bok and Mok cheered.

Mark III said, "Why is everyone cheering?"

And Pam said, "Do you think I could sell my rocks on eBay?"

Later, the aliens held their big ceremony and all the aliens renewed their commitment to their pets. Wilf renewed his commitment to Stuart – and got quite emotional. And Lok got his first ever pet and committed himself to that. Even Alan renewed his commitment to Kevin Phillips.

And then Alan cried into Kevin's fur because yet again he had not managed to destroy the Universe or to become the **RULER OF EVERYTHING**.

Wilf and the SUPREME LEADER of Mars felt so bad for Alan that they found a spare bit of Mars and put a little fence round it and called it '**THE UNIVERSE**' and they told Alan he could be SUPREME LEADER of '**THE UNIVERSE**'. They even put a jar and a suitcase in it to make him feel important.

Wilf and Dot and Stuart said goodbye to their new friends and flew home through the stars and planets – to their own beds and their own pillows and their one moon.

Before they left, the SUPREME LEADER gave Wilf a present for saving Mars. It was the most amazing telescope. With it, Wilf can see Mars and wave to Lok and all his new friends. Except of course, if Dot's been sucking it, then it's jolly difficult to see anything at all.

THE END

Discover more of Wilf's adventures in these brilliant books!

Wilf meets Alan for the first time, and discovers his new next-door neighbour wants to destroy the world with his Big Gun Thingy!

When Alan decides that pirating is an excellent way to destroy the world, Wilf will have to overcome his fear of parrots and walking the plank to save the day...

...Psst! There's more over the page!

1

Alan tries to raise
a scary Animal Army to...
yes, you guessed it...take over the world!
And guess who has to stop him?

wilfthemightyworrier.com